A Bit
More
Than a
Muse

Poetry Blog: www.amazulugaming.com
Instagram: Onepoeticgamer
Twitch: www.twitch.tv/onepoeticgamer

ISBN - 979-8-9857102-2-9

Published by
AmaZulu Gaming, LLC

Cover Art by
Billy Williams, Jr.

Butterfly art work by
Jarred Simmons

Final Edition
Printed in the United States of America

Table of Contents

Out of the Blue

While Butterflies Fly

Analytics Won't Get This

Preface

When she's a bit more than friend but hasn't
recognize his energy yet...or so he thought.

Out of the Blue

Ripple Effects (Like a Butterfly)

Feels affected
by the breath
of the wings of a butterfly
causing this ripple effect
let's, digress on this poetic mix
excuse me miss, I bet it's
a difference since he left
the mess you had to clean up with
bless-ings, no second guess-ing
it appeared to be the worst
until you started heal-ing
self, used pain to find lost wealth
the beauty in your tears
actually started to help
released the feelings felt
just so you know, you are not alone
a quote I picked up off your shelf
for who else but myself
and you know what else,
I've dwelt with
an appreciation for you butterfly
since I can't see you physically
then look into my third eye
recognizing I
feel effects
by the breath
from ripples that now affect
love that's mixed, poetically
thankful you gave me it.

Let Me Be That

Let me be your quiet space
that place you go for comfort
indulging in infinite
resting in endless
withered soul made wet from it
now you can travel round the globe
yet your heart stays here
making you look forward to weekends
like it's Monday,
this love is a holiday worth instant repeat
make your knees get weak
but I'd uplift your feet
til you realize you're in another dimension
you could stand at attention
but let's lay your soles to rest
that way your soul can let
go, I don't know but
I think we can meet in the astral plane
play games like hide and go get
mix, our energies til we find
the number one appealing for the two of us
and I'm just terrestrial, that's extra
flying through space to catch the tear
falling from your face
placed on my heart to
water life back into my system
this rhythm, is much like blues sang
by a songstress named Billie
so let's make this official
from "like" to feeling "just right"

birds of a feather flock together
so you and I flow tight
and, radar beeps reveal the peeps
that emanate from your grace
be that comfort in said space
that quiet found in your place.

Cup of Butter

(or Buttercup)

She rubbed away cares
I had no intentions of letting go
and I flowed in her ambience
wondering if she knows
fully releasing, had been seeking
asylum in places not meant for me
respectfully, not dissing my healing
as my mind moves different then intuition
listening to whispers of those that
always told me they got me
and as I stare aimlessly into sonic waves
she lays on the pressure of
fingertips into my crown
as I now wish on stars
I saw when sneezing hard
hoping she'd look at me
with eyes that speak with
non-verbal communication
maybe she appreciates the foreshadows I sent
like flowers, she could smell the scent
of something smooth like butter
in a cup of poetic verse
let us, check this social distance
kiss without lips despite the desire
to know what beautiful taste like
and I'm like, this is ok right
as I write with the use of black ink
on skin of light.

The Art of Rom

This is me
messaging for customs
artist to artist
or more so
soul to soul,
covering the cost for this
frame of work, for what it's worth
probably can't be priced
wrapped up in the tree of life
your hands transcending lifetimes
reaching me on timelines
and I find, between here
and the lady of the lake
I'll take this chance, this choice
of knotting my technique
locking in on beliefs
that seek truths found drifting
in space, a taste of life
traced around images
with limitless potential
963 hz instrumental surround sound
in backgrounds
as leaves fall down,
happily, peacefully
without a single thought of regret
as the universe lets
us play date through
creation.

While Talking to the Plants

I sit next to plants
amongst those that choose to listen
and I speak about her,
specifically because she is beautiful
in ways not limited to eyesight
or appetite
and despite the fact that distance
is in between
this gives cause to means
of learning on different levels
be that, late night vibes
felt on the inside
or telepathic minds that coincide
let's ballet on these lines
maybe even tell stories
off stage, show case, mic check
a one two, a one two
let's take to
syndicating each other's passion
here's my legion of poems
to your lights, camera, action
note to self, tape the sounds serenaded
from a star seeded deep
in woods beyond just holly
accentuated, contemplative
and before I could get too situated
I glance over at the plants
amongst those that choose to listen
and notice that,
she's been listening
as well.

In Choosing

I've decided
to heal parts of you
which brings light to
areas that need shine
open up the
inner gateway to make way
for that piece of a little better
however you want it
I'm of service
as upon the realization that
we benefit from others experience
when focusing on ifs
that are made into reality
I'm actually quite happy with this
upon release of self
shifts in energy that literally
cause movements, dissolve darkness
make the difference
between sparks that charge hits
to hearts, excuse me while I park Miss
as this is me playing my part
doing something with
no thoughts of return
even though I do yearn
the love of you
in choosing.

Deep Energetics

The taste of strawberries and vanilla
are found between her lips
an abyss of freedom
in which I sink into the depths
meeting universal truths
inside of hips creating this
deep energetic,
experiences beyond feelings
mindgasims,
in other words
bliss has met nirvana
and it gets packaged
in the embodiment
of her.

Jazz Blues (Pt. 2)

You are the mix
of Blue in Green
and in-between the keys
these melodies I play
from soulful influence,
it's the reason I stand in the rain
feeling our fall from grace
upon my face
and here I'll wait
as this is only a moment
placed on repeat
until the tune is in
not ended
recycling after thoughts
to live continuously
complete in me
smoothed out like stones
found crafted by time in rivers
-and-
you are that mix
of Blue and Green
laying patiently in my meditations
unrestricted.

Sky Lights

As I negotiate your focus
let's ponder on
the sunny side of your face
trade places with shadows that
make us appreciate
the art of being
this went from "seeming" to "is"
and that's a bit I'd like to chew
taste the opportunity
pour on some possibilities
and meet me for dinner
at the spot where
we salsa to rhythms
only our souls hear,
and while in that mediation
let's look with our eyes closed
see the big picture
while gazing at the Big Dipper
little do we know
the best could come
and we'd find a way to make it better
that's what is done
when forever is held by freedom
and not control.

Lip Flex

Want that
need that
stretch, that flex
how you get
my attention
listen, I know that
you know that
and this is
borderline ridiculous
got me
feeling feelings
got me
stealing a given
got me
ready and willing
off a flex
let's, not get
to the point that
it's so out of hand
handles will be required
and it's like
that smirk you just gave
has me thinking
you won't cooperate
so I contemplate
on methods that could

counter this
stretch, that flex
which I still desire
to have next.

Smoothie Smooch

She asked if
I wanted a taste of
her strawberry smoothie
in which I partook of
through the use of her straw
and upon finishing my taste test
she made haste to sample
said strawberry smoothie
and said
we basically just kissed
and I spent the rest of the day
enjoying that.

While Butterflies Fly

Art Like

I lay wasted
atop satin sheets
while morning water
colors paint
tinted window curtains.
It's cold in here
despite predictions
of Armageddon
by 12 PM,
I'm walking the maze
of dreams were
you won't leave as promised,
if my soul chose this
my mind doesn't know
the difference
blank canvas is
a color by number
and I already drew
outside the lines
as boundaries are for those
that need direction
and with all this space
between here, now
and then
I'm bound to escape
free to stay in predictions

beneath satin sheets
that I lay wasted in
while morning watercolors paint
my window pain.

Chasing Numbers

I saw her walking
and internalized metaphysically
if by chasing these numbers
she could dial into me
through symmetry and symphonies
sending 7 digits lyrically
repeatedly so she could mentally
feel them through synchrony
then place them in memories
literally, felt spiritual attraction
words speak loud but
she'd rather have action
asked when should I call
11 past but a present suggestion
11 minutes later, unpacked her math then
she spoke frequency as I listened
we triangulated messages
so the angle wouldn't be missing
attention, that we'll be giving
has me thinking of two
lovers that love each other that I'm liking us to
daydreaming, even believing
she is thinking this too
what if I do, comes twice like part duex
I know it could happen as if this was in lieu
but who, would have thought
by a drop of a dime
that somehow, just maybe, in a wrinkle of time

infinitely we'd figure that 8 equals 6+9
our minds shades of grey,
it matters in patters that sign
as we walk directly into souls that cosign.

for H.E.R.
(Poem #28)

The color of love
similar to
the expression of music,
this could be the key to life
or what is meant
by changing one's name
to a symbol,
transcending what was thought
to what is
and I believe this has become
just that
a life changing formation
butterfly metamorphosis
where freedom is found on wings
from change
from love
from life
conversing with the soul
and what I know
is that spoken word
isn't the same as what's written
cause you have the immediate choice
to create the world I have penned
in your mind and heart,
that which your soul
only needed to be reminded of
the beautiful colors
of love.

This Dance

Dance
cause this is paradise
and this feels like
what fine must be right
I'm right next to yours, write
with left-handed hindsight
you seem right-eous
you and I must
use this canvas
paint the stars, thus
His-story plus Her glory seem candy crushed
such, that love can't be confused with lust
touch, can feel your face close
feel your breath stoke
the base of my skin, slowly again
and again, patterned within
the ends of my wits send
vibrations so akin I consent
to let your dark and light in
yang circle back so we can feel yin
indent both cheeks when you grin
and then…then, we begin
this dance.

That's It

Here, it can be seen
our world shared
unabridged, inside out
low key action thriller
with a twist of suspense,
surprises include the words
needing to connect with you
so come a bit closer
in essence
we are already interlocked
through fingers and auras
amplified by the blood moon
hold that position, click it
store that memory for later
present but future self will appreciate that
out of the way
yet somehow in the way
less thinking, more lingering
in depths unlocked
caught, found, intrigued
I believe this is the part we kiss
and whatever comes after
-is-
and that's it.

Resurrected Amour
(Once More)

She blew about in the wind
with rain in her eyes
so I invited her inside
out of the cold
offered these words as warmth
and shouldered her in
the blanket of my soul
I know, I'll play these vibrations in her ear
honed in at 5-2-8…here
as she wiped away tears
I cleared space for her comforts
and as she got comfy
the sunshine began to realign
her mind freeing from the bind
and I, I just listened
making my wishes come true
on the star that just fell into my lap
and just like that
love was reborn.

Intimacy Leaked

This is me
watching you sleep
to enjoy you breathing
quite pleasing
for each request that's seeking
attention given
you don't ask for me to listen
but I do it anyway,
this is me
sharing digitized memories
of things I see
when you're not around
so you can feel a piece
of peace I felt
when left to self,
here's me creating
magic with energy, to keep you safe
put your hand in the place
mine rest when sitting at sunset
watching spirit
can hear it so clearly
it's simply like that
to lay my head in your lap
while you read
lead in with my face
placed on your skin
time within is set without
make the most of it
when musing the comforts of you
having to be brought back to attention

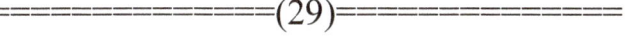

this is me,
writing love letters while at work
then calling you to read them
during lunch
munch on the rhythm
of songs played, as we say
line for line rhymes
while mimicking us being on stage
play the silent game
to see who'll burst first
laugh til it hurts
search a few places
out of the way
so you could have that favorite thing
that familiar taste of love today
a, if I must say
you smell like "good"
enough so I come back
for the scent of you
and, this is me
in intimacy.

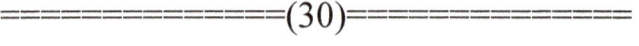

See See

We played coquettishly
I'm thinking we can split between
physical attraction
and spiritual passion
listen, I want to embed this lyrical fetish
until you find me
so we can cuddle our hormones
that'll release oxytocin
when I whisper sweet somethings
into your ear
fingers gently stroking your hair
staring into a pair of eye portals
that switch from mortal
to goddess frequency
and the link between you and me
just got knocked up
from word play,
too late for protection
I'm guessing by the third trimester
we'd have agreed to call her Flowetry
it's a go between
where I'm holding beautiful in one arm
and angelic in the other
so by the time you recover
from being swept off your feet

please note, the clean sweep wasn't fixed
despite being organized by yours truly
one night when he and she
got caught, internet flirting.

Balanced via One

Metaphorically
she shotgun her essence
into my existence
rode high with the assistance
of plant based physics
we became the meta
reflected the word level backwards
so between him and her
it gets no betta
in fact, they better
tell bettors to bank on us
or whatever,
comes from the fall from grace
was based on what they tethered
however, since we're clever enough
to be the others better half
hashtag perceptions don't cost
the sum that's equal of our mass
and antimatter,
no matter what's believed
metaphorically,
she parallels he.

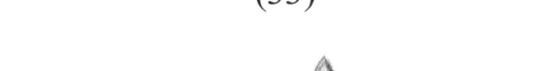

Drive Thru/Us Two

The speaker box attempted
to muffle her attempts in greeting me
and a few seconds after the distortion
her voice carried on the breeze
digitally, I felt at ease
as I believed this to be
the lady I heard before
and what's more
I explored thoughts where
I associated her with a delicate picture
so between my order and driving around this fixture
I placed brain waves on play
thinking of ways
to have her respond to my stimulus
what could bring her to the cusp
of saying something to me
that could open a door
crack a window
give me that inch of opportunity
to present my shot for presentation
no longer complacent
because the brake lights
of the vehicle in front dimmed
and I rimmed my way to the drive thru
to see who or if my intuition was correct
and I was blessed in the gift of her eyes,
lips and nose covered in a mask
and I forgot what I was about to ask
because the task of handing her cash

was paused while I awaited the interaction,
my eyes calculating her math
back of my mind I'm thinking
she's looking just as good as the last
time, she hands me my drink
as I think of ways to ask for her IG identity
and while I ponder, oh I know,
let me play Lights Down Low
that'll show and compose a vibe
damn I can't find the song
and I'm running out of time
before she hands me this meal
and I peel off at a loss for words
at the cost of not being able to find that track
search button, I keep hitting back
and it's in that moment I settle on
J. Bieber questioning where his lady at
what's you E.T.A. sounds play
and I'm like, I guess this is the way
I suppose, maybe I'm doing too much
wondering if I should purpose
a questionnaire, do I take it there
I might strike out if I swing at those
and to my woe, our transaction is now complete
but as I start pulling off she goes
"I like your choice of music…"

Follow the Butterfly

She phased in as an enigma
saying words that came together
as puzzle pieces
I stopped to peep this
should I believe it
or is this another tease that's
just a test for me to guess
let's take this deeper as I digress
stop using brainwaves
instead, let's make soul love
this way thesis and theology
can't bother you or me
what's meant to be will be
as this best kept secret
will be for your eyes only
feel me from the other side of the coast
while coasting down highways
on shifts of thirds
I heard you in the 4th prayer
came to my senses and wrote this
I know I said we aren't using mental
cause this body is rental
and I might need to sit beside you
on the other side of Zion
read that twice
it's a natural occurrence
and currently there's no need for tears
cause I hear you loud and clear
Tri-fold reactions to the harmony

I'm passing, along
I wonder why you stay away so long
after charging me up
what am I to do
but sit between 6 sided spaces
and think of the places this could go
just know, this is me waiting patiently
not anxiously, Masha Allah
for what could be
as I follow this butterfly
curiously.

Analytics Won't Get This

Comforts

I want to comfort you
finding ways in which
pleasure is found beyond a sense
but since this works in the physical element
I flow the opposite of hesitant
so in your feels you get
rub skin with follicles that itch
slow kiss the ways about your stomach
then watch the course of your enjoyment
I want to comfort you,
through necessary means
that find somewhere between
familiar and unexpected
a newness that makes you second guess
if what you currently feel is the best
what could possibly be next
my muse, I have yet to flex
I want to comfort you,
a desire turned obsession
that's turning into an addiction
pictured on milk boxes missing
caught in phonetic constriction
using it as my intervention
listen baby, listen
I want to comfort you
without and within your being
consciously until you're unconsciously seeing
things like angels singing
love that has no meaning

faith inside the seedling
I want to comfort you
in lieu, of who
or what they thought I was suppose to
be the one so we make two
doing things that lovers do
I want-to comfort-you
read to the point I take the lead
pencil lead dulls as I write, it bleeds
metaphor lunch worth twice the read
I want to comfort you
where "until" sits with "forever"
as there you'll find us together
and, I want to comfort you.

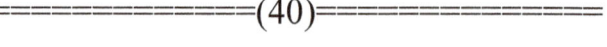

This Is

This is
the should we be doing this
not because it's wrong
but because society tried teaching us
what should be
hinted what could be
but reserved that for those
that have money
and even that's funny because
this is,
something I keep feeling
dreams keep repeating
is it something my soul's needing
as I keep thinking
about you, when not trying to
here you come out the blue
wishing I could learn the lesson
or maybe
this is, the moment waited for
across multi timelines
recreated so I could find
the clue so we combine
memories, internally
emotions through eternity
a love that's always running free
turning around in 360 degrees
and, this is
you and me
finding each other,
again.

Co-Create

I have cosmic feelings for you
all without attachments
essentially pragmatic
it just happens, upon stars
recognized who you are
and forgot about standards, rules
society, one third eyeing me
sideways, this might be it
time to dance without music
these are my confessions
love pure as if adolescent
immaculate in conception
masterpiece while still progressing
focused in on the now moment
as we take action
on positives cycled
in and out
you and I.

When X asked Y

I picked you…
I picked you to remind me
of love forgotten
or more so what it feels like,
placed somewhere between
the birth of time
and the death of it
a bit of that for this
and, I pick you…
this place
that face
this pause, that wait
your ways connected
conversation intersected
mix matched skin tones
integrate then dissected
cookie cut personalities
or actually
it's more like
you get me
I feel you
and it's just so
despite the range
of obvious differences
that when pointed out
make no difference
when what's considered is
souls remembering
when.

It Happens To Be

If my spirit is highly addictive
then get this
shot of frequency to your solar plexus
chakras about to be lit
plugged into the sun
now watch what the moon do with it
I bet you forgot then remembered
what ecstasy is like
without the need of chemicals
this be that vibe in between your temples
can it be all so simple
I find the belief in your dimples
mirror back the same energy and
release that
and here it is
as, your soul is the drug I need.

Etheric Connections

I got in tuned
to feel out the flow of our Divine energy
seamlessly breezing through
this current existence
to see how you manifested
see you in different versions that
lead me to fall in love repeatedly
looking inward so
definitions of unconditional
are recognized as part of the norm
escape limits by out of body experiences
to do a little more than hold your hand
this is me in you, vice versa
self-expression in reflections
imagining reality that's actually
being awake in the dream
lean in for the close up
as the show begins you'll find twins
causing one to see double
wax these windows til moonlight appears
hope she takes it personal
-objectively-
blog it in space amongst stars
make our vibe go from universal to multi-
express truth in different formats
that rid us of exclusive
so here's to this
human connection via soul link

a toast where we drink from the pools
that flow from one another
on our journey through this thing
called life.

Learning Who

Night lights flow to this verse
sitting half and half on
what could be
dreams are big in comparison to reality
where I sit two galaxies away
staring at you,
anticipating details that might entail
thoughts and feelings held captive
I seek to release, considering a bit too much
contemplating that she's got to see
I ride the vibe that says I'm feeling her
the way she moves, the attitude
we could rock this groove together
however, despite assumptions
late afternoon walks and random chit chat
I find that I'm paused in speculation
a hope distances from kissing your cheek
caressing your feet
or sniffing what's beneath the armor you wear
I care enough to respect boundaries
but wishing I could fit somewhere
between held hands, a chance
and the possibility of learning you
if you so choose
pardon me if I seem rude
but if thick thighs save lives
come save mine and be my heroine
switch places and I could be the same thing
only difference being,

we're human beings that replace capes
with interlaced soul strings
a love thang, that brings us to the point
off the pitch, inhaled this equivalent of a joint
let's anoint our opportunity, see what it do
got me asking, what say you?

Chakra Art

Wind kissed after she dreamt this
much like
tear bliss when my heart thought it
she defended
when I descended
I found myself so
flames could mend splits,
this isn't scripted
my spirit lifted
perspective shifted
poetic gifted
and she,
she…she's reminiscent
those eyes, hips
I can't forget memories at distant
reincarnated as goddess
similar to fantasies my soul witnessed
and somehow it seems
there is unfinished business
so with persistence I send this
through sub consciousness
in balance
that's three 2s
one poetic-jitsu
it's finished.

Chameleon Description

No filter
for this picture
that draws upon allure,
in maturity
tickling a fancy
I held in reserve for
no one in particular
maybe until
unexpectedly you stepped
across lines drawn in sand
without the double dare
extended this gift
like long lashes
eyeing opportunity
that could be, may be
I don't know for sure
but your style
I'm unearthing
down to your hair follicles
naturally, like reefs
this poem inked
into skin
I'm wondering
if your cheeks are imprinted
into my head
since you've been sitting
on my mind for
a long stretch
and I bet

you'd like this
investment of time
spent on a rose
that's a shoulder above the rest
if you let
the music play what's left
of our song
you and I might just
get to play
in tune.

Here, With Hugs Waiting

Here, with hugs waiting
until your return
from what ever, where ever
to give this
to give it
unto you.
Here, with hugs waiting
with tears building in lids
for a release that's given
on the very sight of you
repeating the first time
as if it's been a long while
cause I'm
here, with hugs, waiting
learning through dreams
creating from feels
needing all of which
is you, hoping
when you get here
there'll be hugs
for me too.

Oh, By The Way

She loves without reason
and despite me being in agreeance
sometimes what my mind is seeing
is clogged with disbelief
I'm freeing, these restrictions
listen to intuition, wishing on a star
not falling, but feeling our celestial friendship
imagination endless, processing through dreams to
find relief
of pressure, not knowing whether
this ends together, however
whatever's clever is not
the answer that I seek
so here's the reposition
and, oh, by the way
I'm in love with you.

About The Author

Billy Williams, Jr. was born to write poetry.
Poetically knows as B-Dot and OnePoeticGamer,
the life as a poet all started because of a girl back in
7th grade. Seeing he had a gift with words, he began
to use his energy to produce poetry that spoke to
various genres.

Hailing from Raleigh, North Carolina, Billy is a
poet, educator, coach, gamer, streamer and
motivator. A Bit More Than a Muse is Billy's
eighth book of published poetry, with more poetry
books to be released in the near future.

If you want to find out more information about Billy's upcoming books, you can contact him by way of e-mail at onepoeticgamer@amazulugaming.com or sending a message to him from the following website www.amazulugaming.com. If you wish to know more about his gaming/streaming life, check him at www.twitch.tv/onepoeticgamer.

Social Media Contacts

Poetry Blog: www.amazulugaming.com
Instagram: Onepoeticgamer
Twitch: www.twitch.tv/onepoeticgamer

AmaZulu Gaming, LLC

Poetry Books Written By One Poetic

Poetic Superhero

Everybody is looking for a hero. Poetic Superhero is here for you.

The I prElude I

In order to find we, HE must find himself before finding SHE.

His Emotions Released

This is written for Her…I'm glad I finally got Her attention.

School Dad

Poetry inspired by 16 years of working as an educator in elementary, middle and high school.

the Book of HER

33 poems for HER.

The Poetic Verse - My Book of Rhymes

When I feel the flow, I let go with words.

Excommunicated (A Bard's Tale)

Exit wounds given by another can lead to one's salvation.

A Bit More Than a Muse

When she's a bit more than friend but hasn't recognize his energy yet...or so he thought.

<u>Spoken Word By One Poetic</u>

A Story of a Starseed
(upcoming 2023)

www.ingramcontent.com/pod-product-compliance
Lightning Source LLC
Chambersburg PA
CBHW042145170626
46815CB00006BA/320